# Newcastle
## CITY COUNCIL

## Education and Libraries Directorate

### Newcastle Libraries & Information Service

Please return or renew this item by the last date shown. Books can be renewed at the library, by post or by telephone if not reserved by another reader.

| Due for return | Due for return | Due for return |
| --- | --- | --- |
| | | |
| | | |
| | | |
| | | |
| | | |
| | | |
| | | |
| | | |
| | | |
| | | |
| | | |
| | | |
| | | |
| | | |

E4331/144

Ladybird

It hides, back inside.
Somebody's coming.

It's Mrs Lady.

Spots the box,
starts to smile.
Winds the handle.
Waits for a while.

Tick, tick, tick…

It's a jack-in-the-box.
What a springy zingy thing!

tick
tick

BOING!

Mrs Lady spring-a-zing-zings.
Somebody's coming.

It's Brother and Sister.
Mrs Lady shows them the trick,
turns the handle… click, click, click.

Tick, tick, tick, tick, tick.

tick
tick

Sister turns the handle –
click, click, **click**,
grins at the others.

Tick, tick, tick, tick, tick, tick, tick…

tick
tick

Brother turns the handle
round and round.
The handle unwinds
with a tick-tick sound…
Tick, tick, tick, tick, tick, tick,
tick, tick, tick…

tick
tick

# BOING-BEDOING!

Bouncing higher, higher than before.
Jumping with the jack, zingy-springing
off the floor. Bounce! Bounce! Boy-oing!

Goodbye Mrs Lady.
Goodbye Brother and Sister.